ANIMAL Lingo

by Pam Conrad
paintings by Barbara Bustetter Falk

 A Laura Geringer Book
An Imprint of HarperCollins*Publishers*

I would like to acknowledge
the generosity and special linguistic talents of
Dasa Redmond, Marina Berti, Carole Crowe,
John Gillooley, Barbara Fritz, Carol Dahl, Masako Stampf,
Peter Matthiessen, Pnina Kass, Jenni Niittyla, and
John Lucy's Irish mother-in-law.

Animal Lingo
Text copyright © 1995 by Pam Conrad
Illustrations copyright © 1995 by Barbara Bustetter Falk
Printed in Mexico. All rights reserved.

Library of Congress Cataloging-in-Publication Data
Conrad, Pam.
    Animal lingo / by Pam Conrad ; paintings by Barbara Bustetter Falk.
        p.   cm.
    "A Laura Geringer book."
    Summary: Provides the words different languages use for a variety of
animal sounds.
    ISBN 0-06-023401-6. — ISBN 0-06-023402-4 (lib. bdg.)
    1. Onomatopoeia—Juvenile literature.   2. Animal sounds—Juvenile
literature.   [1. Sounds, Words for.   2. Animal sounds.]   I. Falk, Barbara
Bustetter, ill.   II. Title.
P119.C66   1995   93-22163
418—dc20   CIP
                                                         AC

Typography by Tom Starace
1   2   3   4   5   6   7   8   9   10
❖
First Edition

In Great Neck, where the writers
gather 'round a bowl of nuts, they
go on and on and on. . . .

For Johanna Hurwitz, my hero

—P.C.

For Alyssa

—B.B.F

In Old Czechoslovakia, where the sun rises from the Morava River and shines on the corn, the rooster says:

Ki-ki-ri-co!

In Holland, where the bicycles roll along the red-brick paths, the cows say:

 *Booo.*

In Ireland, in County Longford on the road to Drumlish, the lamb says:

Maa-aa-aa.

In Venezuela, on a small ranch in the highlands, the pig says:

Jui. Jui.

In America, where Old Mill Pond meets Sunrise Highway, the goose says:

Honk!

In the Yukon, when the ice begins to crack and melt, the raven says:

Klawk!

In Japan, beside the door to the garden, the cat whispers:

In China, on the bridge
below Nan-p'ing Mountain,
the horses' hooves go:

Geh-deng,
geh-deng,
geh-deng.

In Russia, beneath the leaf of a huge purple cabbage, the frog says:

Cua. Cua.

In Tanzania, on a
path through the
Olduvai Gorge, the
wildebeest says:

Blart!

In Turkey, along the sea at the foot of the Northern Mountains, the dogs say:

Hav! Hav!

In Israel, beside the
Sea of Galilee, the
turkey says:

Holderolderol.

In Finland, beneath a tender birch tree that shines in the dusk, the duck says:

Kvaak! Kvaak!

But all over the world, when night settles on the rooftops, children say: